BOXER
FUN IS OUR BUSINESS

www.booksbyboxer.com

Bee Three Books

Bee Three Publishing is an imprint of Books By Boxer
Published by
Books By Boxer, Leeds, LS13 4BS, UK
Books by Boxer (EU), Dublin, D02 P593, IRELAND
Boxer Gifts LLC, 955 Sawtooth Oak Cir, VA 22802, USA

cs@boxer.gifts

MADE IN CHINA
ISBN: 9781915410993

MIX
Paper
FSC FSC™ C007683

This book is produced from responsibly sourced paper to ensure forest management

I'd follow you anywhere...

but sometimes I wish I

had asked where we're

going FIRST!

We hold hands and dance through life... and I'm never LETTING GO!

We've been friends for so long I can't remember which of us is the BAD INFLUENCE!

No matter what....

we never ever

WASTE WINE.

You always help me up when I fall... once you've STOPPED LAUGHING!

You bring out the best in me... and also the **WORST!**

I thought I was normal
until I met my
BEST FRIEND!

I'm not afraid to try new things... because you're usually **WORSE**!

Some people think we're weird... but we just know how to **HAVE FUN!**

We'd be the world's best popstars... **IF ONLY WE COULD SING!**

You're the friend that makes ME look like...

THE NORMAL ONE!

Best friends: they know how crazy you are...

yet still choose to be seen in public with you.

We never need to look
for a PLUS ONE!

Together we're crazy.
It's the only thing
that keeps us SANE!

We're friends because we're the same amount of **WEIRD.**

You're the reason my sides hurt from laughing

TOO MUCH!

You fill my heart with joy, and my stomach with WINE!

Friends bring happiness...
best friends bring WINE!

You never let me do stupid things...

ALONE!

We've survived heartbreaks, bad haircuts, and questionable fashion – THAT'S REAL FRIENDSHIP.

You and I are proof that two wrongs **DO** make a **RIGHT!**

They say you can't pick your family, but lucky for me, I PICKED YOU.

All of my best nights are spent with you – even the ones that are HAZY!

You're the friend who makes me laugh at the most...

INAPPROPRIATE
TIMES.

You make boring days fun and fun days...

UNFORGETTABLE.

You're not just my friend;
you're my unpaid
LIFE COACH!

Every shopping spree turns into our very own **CATWALK.**

Our shenanigans would make the perfect **SITCOM!**

We're like a comedy duo that forgot to rehearse. Yet somehow, we're HILARIOUS TOGETHER!

You're my excuse to eat dessert even when we promised to 'BE GOOD'.

If I were a rich celebrity,
I'd still let you hang out
with me.

You've seen me at my worst, yet you still

STICK AROUND!

We're going to be friends forever...

YOU KNOW TOO MUCH!

Best friends don't

just know your story,

they helped **WRITE IT!**

I was innocent until you CAME ALONG!

You're my best friend because no one else would deal with my crazy for this long.

I'm not saying you're a bad influence, but I'm never in trouble when I'm alone...

You hold me up... until we fall down LAUGHING!

You're my favorite person to make fun of, but if anyone else does it, they're

GOING DOWN!

We're like the perfect recipe: a little bit of chaos, a whole lot of love, and just the right amount of **BAD DECISIONS.**

We'll be friends til we're old and senile, then we'll become NEW FRIENDS AGAIN!

You're the reason I have

CROW'S FEET!

Friends give compliments...
best friends tell you the
TRUTH!

We can stay up all night talking...

until we can't talk

ANYMORE!

We don't need an occasion to celebrate, our friendship is **ENOUGH!**

Our friendship should come with a WARNING LABEL!

You bring the wine...

I'll bring the cake!

They say friends are like bras – supportive and close to your heart. But let's be honest, we're more like

MISMATCHED SOCKS.

Friendship is about being embarrassing in public, and

NOT CARING!

You're the friend I can call when I need someone to help me bury the evidence.

Our friendship is like wine, it only gets BETTER WITH AGE.

We don't judge each other.
We judge... TOGETHER!

We go together like

COFFEE AND CAKE!

Whatever the weather,
we'll be out TOGETHER!

I don't know what I'd do without you...

but I'm sure it would
involve way less laughter
and a lot more sanity!

If I had a dollar for every time you made me laugh, I'd be rich enough to hire us a chauffeur.

I know I can always count on you to be just as unprepared for life as I am.

When I say I won't tell anybody, my best friend DOESN'T COUNT!

You are my
PARTNER IN CRIME!

Having fun with you is
ALL THE THERAPY
I NEED!

If we ever end up in jail together, just know it was your idea, and I

FULLY SUPPORTED IT.

You're there for me during my highest of highs...

and lowest of lows.

We're the perfect mix of CLASSY AND SASSY!

You're proof that good taste in friends is a skill, **NOT AN ACCIDENT.**

We always start with good intentions...
and end up with stories we can't tell anyone!

We'll always be the last at the bar – but we only need **OURSELVES!**

We're like coffee and cream...

different, but we're

BETTER TOGETHER!

Our friendship is built on wine, sass, and SHENANIGANS!

Spontaneous plans with you are my FAVORITE kind of plans.

A friend is what the heart needs ALL THE TIME.

Our friendship is supporting each other's questionable

LIFE CHOICES!

All our ideas are good ideas... even the

BAD ONES!

You're like my therapist, but cheaper, funnier, and way less judgmental about my **LIFE CHOICES.**

You understand that my 5 minutes is...

CLOSER TO 30!

Our friendship has saved me a fortune in

THERAPY.

We're the type of friends who can spend hours talking about absolutely

NOTHING!

You're the friend who will laugh when I trip over my own feet, then **PICK ME UP!**

You and I are more than friends... we're a **DUO!**

You're the one who talks me out of dumb ideas...

and then helps me pull them off anyway.

The only way to have a friend is to BE ONE!

We may not have it all together, but together, WE HAVE IT ALL...

I'm SO lucky to have a friend LIKE YOU!